A Note to Parents

DK READERS is a compelling program for beginning readers, designed in conjunction with leading literacy experts, including Dr. Linda Gambrell, Professor of Education at Clemson University. Dr. Gambrell has served as President of the International Reading Association, National Reading Conference, and College Reading Association.

Beautiful illustrations and superb full-color photographs combine with engaging, easy-to-read stories and informational texts to offer a fresh approach to each subject in the series. Each DK READER is guaranteed to capture a child's interest while developing his or her reading skills, general knowledge, and love of reading.

The five levels of DK READERS are aimed at different reading abilities, enabling you to choose the books that are exactly right for your child:

Pre-level 1: Learning to read

Level 1: Beginning to read

Level 2: Beginning to read alone

Level 3: Reading alone

Level 4: Proficient readers

The "normal" age at which a child begins to read can be anywhere from three to eight years old. Adult participation through the lower levels is very helpful for providing encouragement, discussing storylines, and sounding out unfamiliar words.

No matter which level you select, you can be sure that you are helping your child learn to read, then read to learn!

LONDON, NEW YORK, MUNICH,
MELBOURNE, AND DELHI

For Dorling Kindersley
Senior Editor Alastair Dougall
Editorial Assistant Jo Casey
Designer Sandra Perry
Brand Manager Rob Perry
Publishing Manager Simon Beecroft
Category Publisher Alex Allan
Production Controller Kara Wallace
Production Editor Sean Daly

Reading Consultant
Linda B. Gambrell, Ph.D.

First published in the United States in 2009 by
DK Publishing
375 Hudson Street
New York, New York, 10014
018
11 12 10 9 8 7 6 5 4 3
DD530—04/09

DK Books are available at special discounts when purchased in bulk
for sales promotions, premiums, fund-raising, or educational use.
For details, contact: DK Publishing Special Markets, 375 Hudson
Street, New York, New York 10014
SpecialSales@dk.com

Published in Great Britain by Dorling Kindersley Limited.

A catalog record for this book
is available from the Library of Congress.

ISBN: 978-0-7566-4532-8 (Hardback)
ISBN: 978-0-7566-4531-1 (Paperback)

Color reproduction by Alta Image, UK
Printed and bound by L-Rex, China

Discover more at
www.dk.com

Contents

PROFICIENT
4
READERS

THE STORY OF WOLVERINE

Written by Michael Teitelbaum

Fighting machine
Wolverine's mutant abilities make him a perfect fighting machine.

Mutants
Mutants are individuals born with special abilities. Wolverine's include an amazing self-healing power.

Introduction

The mutant who has come to be called Wolverine is the best at what he does. But what he does isn't pretty! He's a complicated individual. At times he is brooding and quiet. At other times he's intense and violent. Always, he struggles to control his basic animal instincts which tell him to kill and destroy.

But what exactly is it that he does? Quite simply, he fights. And he fights more fiercely and skillfully than almost anyone else. Don't let his small size fool you.

Wolverine's mutant abilities,
animal instincts, and razor-sharp
claws make him almost unstoppable.
He spent years living alone in the
wild like an animal. He fought in
military units and went on secret spy
missions. He's always this close to
giving in to uncontrollable rage. At
heart he's a loner, yet he's best
known as a member of the famous
mutant team the X-Men.

Early days

John Howlett
James's father was cold and unaffectionate.

Dog and Rose
His friendship with Dog and Rose made James happy.

It may surprise you to learn that Wolverine is more than 100 years old! His real name is James Howlett and he was born in the late 1800s in Alberta, Canada. James was the second son of wealthy landowners John and Elizabeth Howlett. However, growing up on a big estate with rich parents did not provide young James with an easy life.

His mother spent time in a mental institution, following the death of her oldest son, John Jr. His father was distant. As a boy, James spent much of his time on the Howlett estate with two companions.

They were a girl named Rose and a boy nicknamed "Dog." Dog was the son of Thomas Logan, the groundskeeper on the estate.

A great tragedy led to the accidental discovery of James's mutant power. Thomas Logan attempted to kidnap James's mother Elizabeth. When James's father, John, came to her defense, Logan shot him dead. Seeing this sent young James into a rage. Claws suddenly extended from the backs of his hands. He drove off the intruder but watched in horror as his mother took her own life.

Thomas Logan
The shady groundskeeper could have been James's real father.

Elizabeth Howlett
Experiencing the death of his mother was very traumatic.

Living among the wolves
Logan's mutant abilities helped him survive in the wild.

Toughened by the mines
Working at the mining colony toughened Logan's body.

Logan the drifter

Unable to deal with the horrors he had witnessed, James fled the Howlett estate. He was frightened and confused by the strange claws that had sprung from his hands. He was also terrified of the uncontrollable rage he had felt. He took the name Logan to hide his true identity and became a drifter. Although he didn't know it at the time, James's power to heal quickly protected his young mind from the horrors he had lived through.

As a result, James's true origin and identity remained a secret, even from him, for many years. Even when he eventually joined the X-Men as Wolverine, he had no idea of his true past.

During his life on the run, James, now known as Logan, had many adventures. He worked in a mining colony and lived as a wild beast in the woods among the wolves. He fought in both World War I and World War II, and lived in Japan as a samurai. He lived on the island of Madripoor, a haven for smugglers and pirates. He even worked as a spy for the C.I.A. before the Canadian government found him.

C.I.A. spy
Logan's heightened senses made him a great spy.

In Japan, Wolverine learned the fighting skills of the samurai.

Professor Thorton

Professor Thorton started what would become the Weapon X project just after World War II. He based his project on the work of the geneticist Mister Sinister.

The incredibly hard metal adamantium was grafted onto Wolverine's bones, giving him a powerful, unbreakable skeleton. His mutant healing ability enabled Wolverine to survive the procedure.

Weapon X

A secret Canadian government project known as Weapon X was trying to create a super-soldier. Agents of Weapon X kidnapped Logan. They planned to graft a skeleton onto his bones made of an indestructible metal known as adamantium. Weapon X felt Logan was the perfect candidate for this procedure because his mutant healing ability would allow him to survive the brutal operation.

Following the operation, Weapon X agents tried to brainwash Logan to do their bidding. But their attempts at mind control failed and drove Logan insane. He escaped from them and lived like an animal in the Canadian wilderness.

He was found by James and Heather Hudson, agents of Department H, a secret Canadian research and intelligence agency.

Deadpool

Silver Fox

Sabretooth

Other mutants
Other mutants used by the Weapon X project include Deadpool, Silver Fox, and Sabretooth.

Joining the X-Men

When James Hudson heard about the American Super Hero team called the Fantastic Four, he decided to form a Canadian hero team. Called Alpha Flight, this strike force would be made up of the most powerful heroes in Canada. Hudson wanted Wolverine to be the leader of this new team.

Professor X
Wolverine felt safe at Professor X's School for Gifted Youngsters.

Many mutants
Wolverine met many other mutants who had difficult lives because of their abilities.

However, Wolverine was about to meet a man who would change his life forever: Wolverine met Professor Charles Xavier, leader of the X-Men team of mutant Super Heroes. Xavier, also known as Professor X, immediately recognized that Wolverine was a mutant and asked Wolverine to join the X-Men.

Wolverine agreed, refusing Hudson's offer to lead Alpha Flight. He was glad to join a team of fellow mutants. At Professor X's school Wolverine had found a home at last.

X-Men school
Mutants learned to control their abilities at Professor X's school.

Hero team
Wolverine has fought many battles alongside the X-Men.

Adamantium claws
Wolverine's claws can be deadly weapons.

Agility
Wolverine uses his great agility to swiftly dodge attacks.

Wolverine's abilities

Wolverine's mutant abilities combine to make him a perfect fighting machine. His amazing healing ability allows him to recover from injuries in seconds. It also makes him immune to poison, resistant to disease, and accounts for his unusually long life.

His healing ability also made it possible for the scientists of the Weapon X project to attach a skeleton to his bones made of the super-strong metal adamantium. This metal skeleton makes him even more resistant to attack and it gave him his amazing metal claws. They spring from his hands and can slice through almost anything.

Wolverine also has enhanced endurance and agility, allowing him to fight longer, harder, and more skillfully than almost any opponent. His senses of sight, hearing, and smell are also amazingly sharp and are more like those of an animal than a human being. Wolverine can see things far away, hear faint sounds in the distance, and identify an object or enemy by scent alone.

Add all these things up, and you can see why Wolverine is almost unbeatable in a fight.

Quick recovery
Wolverine recovers from injury very quickly, and is ready to rejoin the fight.

Wolverine struggles with Agent Zero, who can fire concussion blasts from his hands.

Professor X

Professor Charles Xavier is the man responsible for making Wolverine part of the X-Men team. The professor is one of the most powerful mutants in the world, with amazing mental powers. He can read minds, send messages into the minds of others or erase people's memories. He can also use his mutant power to temporarily paralyze people or knock them out with powerful mental bolts.

Xavier realized that there were many other mutants in the world so he started a school called Xavier's School for Gifted Youngsters.

Answers
Professor X helped Wolverine in his search for information about his hidden past.

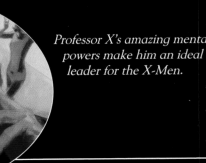

Professor X's amazing mental powers make him an ideal leader for the X-Men.

His students at the school call him Professor X. At this school, young mutants learn to control their powers and use them for good. Professor X believes that humans and mutants should live and work together peacefully. He teaches this philosophy at his school.

When Wolverine arrived, he became a valuable part of the X-Men team. He also became a teacher and mentor to many of the young mutants at the school.

Cerebro
Cerebro is Professor X's super computer, helping Professor X find mutants all over the world.

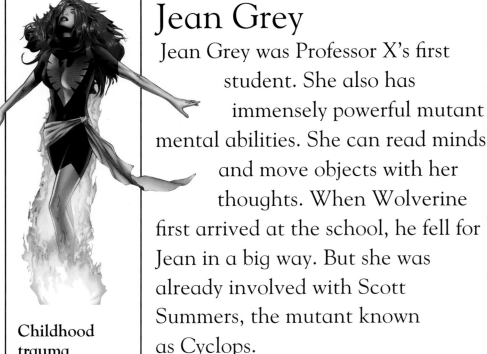

Jean Grey

Jean Grey was Professor X's first student. She also has immensely powerful mutant mental abilities. She can read minds and move objects with her thoughts. When Wolverine first arrived at the school, he fell for Jean in a big way. But she was already involved with Scott Summers, the mutant known as Cyclops.

The Phoenix Force is a powerful cosmic being that created a duplicate Jean Grey.

Childhood trauma
Witnessing her friend's death activated Jean's mutant powers.

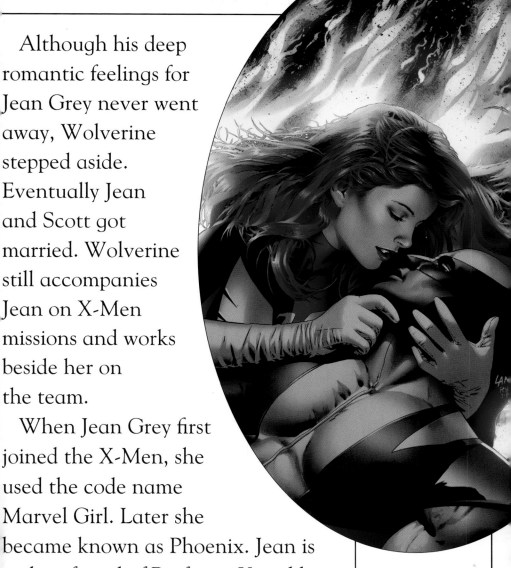

Although his deep romantic feelings for Jean Grey never went away, Wolverine stepped aside. Eventually Jean and Scott got married. Wolverine still accompanies Jean on X-Men missions and works beside her on the team.

When Jean Grey first joined the X-Men, she used the code name Marvel Girl. Later she became known as Phoenix. Jean is a close friend of Professor X and he values her advice. She remains a close friend to Wolverine as well, although he still wishes they could be more than just friends. Together they have battled evil mutants and aliens threatening Earth.

Partners
Wolverine knows in his heart that his love for Jean Grey will only remain a dream.

Rogue

Many of the younger X-Men at Professor X's School for Gifted Youngsters look up to Wolverine as a kind of big brother, and none more so than Rogue.

Her mutant ability first showed itself when she was a teenager. If she touches someone, she absorbs that person's memories and abilities. This process leaves the other person unconscious and can sometimes cause them serious injury. If the person is another mutant, Rogue will absorb his or her powers.

Imagine going through life never able to touch another person. That is Rogue's fate. Because of this, her teenage years were very lonely.

Ms. Marvel
Rogue once touched the hero known as Ms. Marvel, gaining her powers of invulnerability, super strength, and flight.

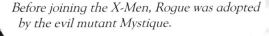

Before joining the X-Men, Rogue was adopted by the evil mutant Mystique.

But, like so many other mutants, including Wolverine, Rogue found a home at Professor X's school.

While others shied away from Rogue, Wolverine befriended her. He looks out for her and protects her from evil mutants who would do her harm.

Teamwork
Wolverine and Rogue make a good team, and often fight battles together as part of the X-Men.

Nightcrawler

Some mutants, like Wolverine, can hide the fact that they are different from normal humans. Some, like Nightcrawler, cannot.

Nightcrawler's mother is Mystique. He inherited his blue skin from her. He also has pointy ears and a tail. Ordinary people have always been afraid of him.

Nightcrawler's mutant power enables him to instantly teleport himself from one place to another. He is also a skilled acrobat.

Raised by gypsy circus performers, Nightcrawler became a high-wire and trapeze artist.

Vanished
One second Nightcrawler is there, and then he's gone!

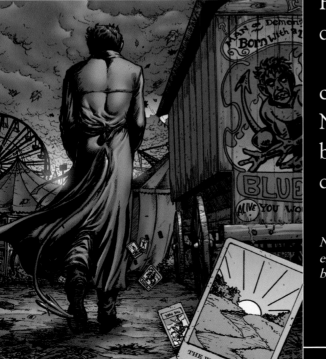

Nightcrawler's tail is strong enough to support his entire body weight.

Nightcrawler's power to transport himself didn't hurt his ability to put on a great acrobatic circus show.

When he accidentally killed his best friend, the son of a fellow circus performer, Nightcrawler was hunted down by an angry mob. They called him a demon because of his appearance and chased him with revenge in their hearts.

Nightcrawler was saved by Professor X, who used his mutant telepathic powers to stop the crowd. A grateful Nightcrawler joined the X-Men.

Acrobat
Nightcrawler was a skilled circus performer.

Nightcrawler and Wolverine became friends and fought many battles together.

Guardian
James Hudson,
known as
Guardian, is
the leader of
Alpha Flight.

**Other
members**
Major
Mapleleaf,
Nemesis,
Northstar,
Centennial,
and Yukon
Jack have
also served in
Alpha Flight.

Alpha Flight

When the Canadian government
wanted to form its own team of
Super Heroes, they turned to
James MacDonald Hudson.
Hudson was a great engineer and
inventor. He created an
electromagnetic battlesuit for himself
and became the hero Guardian.

Snowbird

Sasquatch

Shaman

Aurora

Guard

Puck

Puck II

Wolverine

Hudson's suit allowed Guardian to fly and shoot bolts of electromagnetic force. It also protected him with a force field.

Hudson recruited Shaman, a Native American mystic, Sasquatch, a man who transforms into a monster, Snowbird, who can change into any Arctic animal, and Puck, a trained fighter and acrobat.

Right from the start, Hudson had one man in mind to be the leader of Alpha Flight—Wolverine. However, Wolverine rejected the offer to lead Alpha Flight and chose to join the X-Men instead.

Vindicator
James's wife, Heather, joined Alpha Flight as the hero Vindicator.

Teams
Members of the New Avengers come from other teams such as the Fantastic Four and the X-Men.

New Avengers

When the Super Villain Electro helped stage a break-out at the Raft, a maximum security prison, a group of heroes joined together to stop them. Spider-Woman, Luke Cage, Spider-Man, Captain America, and Iron Man were joined by Wolverine, who was on a break from the X-Men.

The Super Villain Electro has often battled the New Avengers.

And so the New Avengers were formed. Over 40 Super Villains escaped from the Raft, including Sauron, a half-human, half-dinosaur creature. Wolverine's tracking skills were a great help to the team and so were his fighting abilities.

Wolverine helped the team track Sauron to the Savage Lands, a tropical region of Antarctica where dinosaurs still roam. When Sauron was eventually recaptured, Captain America decided to keep the New Avengers together.

When Captain America discovered a conspiracy to hide Super Villains thought to be dead, he once again called on Wolverine. In time, however, Wolverine returned to the X-Men.

Great heroes
Spider-Man, Iron Man, and Captain America joined the team, too.

Sauron
Sauron has razor-sharp claws and the ability to breathe fire.

Nick Fury and S.H.I.E.L.D.

The secret government agency known as S.H.I.E.L.D. (Supreme Headquarters International Espionage Law-enforcement Division) was formed in response to the threat of Hydra. Hydra is a worldwide, high-tech organization dedicated to world domination.

When S.H.I.E.L.D. was formed, the government asked Nick Fury, a World War II hero, to head up the agency. In addition to being a natural leader, Fury also had many contacts in the Super Hero community.

Fury-ous
Sergeant Nick Fury, a decorated soldier, was invited to head up S.H.I.E.L.D.

Hydra is a global terrorist organization out to destroy all Super Heroes.

The people who started S.H.I.E.L.D. knew that the organization would be facing threats from various criminal groups on Earth. But they also knew that S.H.I.E.L.D. would have to combat extraterrestrial attacks. When danger threatens from outer space, it's always handy to have Super Heroes on your team!

Nick Fury brought in Wolverine. Fury appreciated Wolverine's fighting ability, tracking skills, and his past training as a secret agent.

S.H.I.E.L.D.
The identity of the people who started S.H.I.E.L.D. remains unknown. S.H.I.E.L.D. headquarters is a mobile helicarrier. It also has offices in all major cities.

Sabretooth

Wolverine was not the only mutant taken by the Weapon X project. A mutant named Victor Creed, who came to be called Sabretooth, was also experimented on by Weapon X scientists.

Sabretooth has the same basic mutant abilities as Wolverine. He has super-fast healing power, immunity to disease, incredibly sharp senses of sight, smell, and hearing, and exceptionally long life. It is believed that Sabretooth is as old, if not older, than Wolverine.

Ferocious
Sabretooth remains alert, always ready to attack.

Sabretooth, like Wolverine, also had horrible childhood.

Victor Creed was a member of C.I.A.'s strike force, Team X.

Sabretooth, too, lived as a wild beast in the woods. But, unlike Wolverine, he has never been tamed. While Wolverine constantly struggles to keep his savage, animalistic side in check, Sabretooth embraces it. He's an uncontrollable monster without a shred of humanity left within him.

No one in the world has as much in common with Wolverine as Sabretooth, and yet the two remain the most bitter of enemies.

Sabretooth worked for the Hellfire Club, a group of mutants bent on world domination.

Magneto

Magneto, the master of magnetism, is the X-Men's greatest enemy. Ironically, he was once a close friend of Professor X. However, the two share opposite beliefs. As soon as the world became aware of the existence of mutants, many people feared them. This led to bigotry and the belief among many that mutants should be carefully controlled and watched.

Professor X has always believed in working for human-mutant cooperation; Magneto believes that the only way to prevent humans from oppressing mutants is to conquer the human race.

Opposites attract
Magneto and Professor X used to be good friends.

Magneto wears his helmet to help keep Professor X from reading or controlling his mind.

Magneto believes that mutants are superior to humans and should rule over them. This clash of views has led to many conflicts between Wolverine and his fellow X-Men, and Magneto.

Magneto formed the Brotherhood of Evil Mutants and enlisted fellow mutants Toad, Mystique, Mastermind, and Quicksilver to help him battle the X-Men. Later he formed a new band of mutants called the Acolytes, who share his belief in mutant domination over humans.

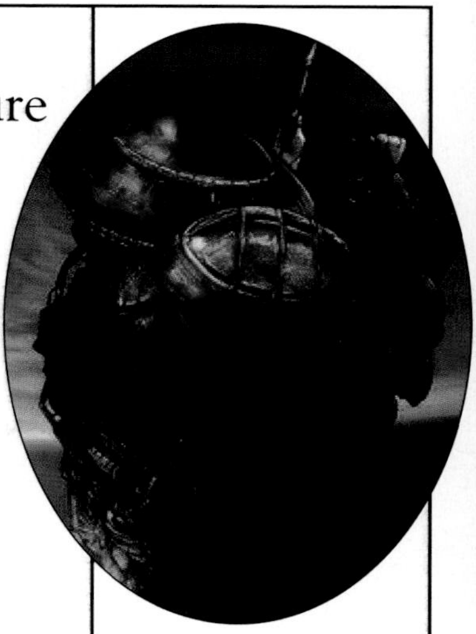

Asteroid M
Asteroid M, a giant asteroid that orbits the Earth, was one of Magneto's home bases. He later moved to his own island, called Genosha.

Magneto's Brotherhood of Evil Mutants often battled the X-Men.

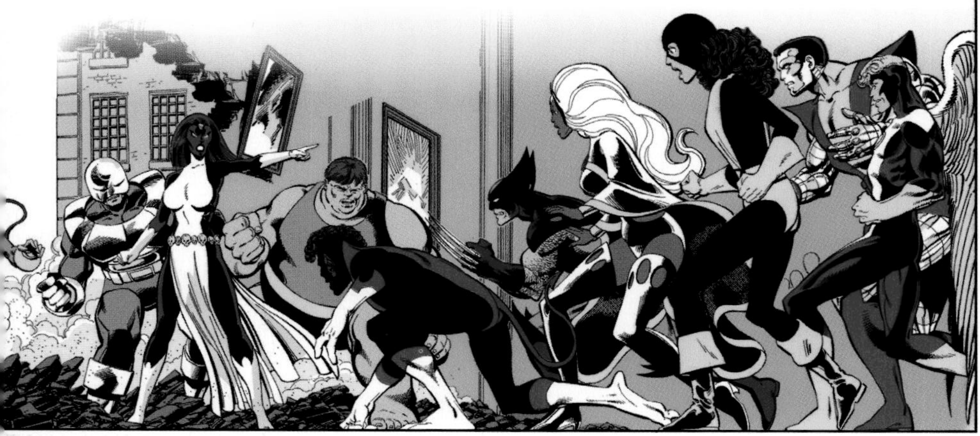

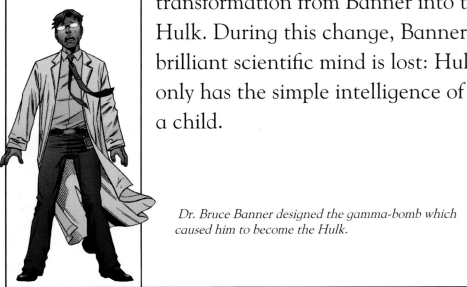

Hulk

Perhaps the only being who can match Wolverine for sheer fury and rage is the Hulk. Start with his huge size and enormous strength. Add to that the anger that fuels his very being and you've got one mean, green fighting machine. Caught in a gamma-bomb blast, Dr. Bruce Banner became the Hulk. It is anger that triggers his transformation from Banner into the Hulk. During this change, Banner's brilliant scientific mind is lost: Hulk only has the simple intelligence of a child.

Ripped
Bruce Banner becomes the Hulk.

Dr. Bruce Banner designed the gamma-bomb which caused him to become the Hulk.

When confronted with a problem, Hulk simply smashes whatever gets in his way. More than once, Wolverine has opposed him and the pair have fought many epic battles. They have sometimes worked together as members of the Avengers Super Hero team, but generally they would prefer to avoid each other.

The Avengers
The Hulk sometimes works with the Avengers, a Super Hero team.

Power vs. power
It's Wolverine's claws and fury against the Hulk's strength and rage in a battle of pure power.

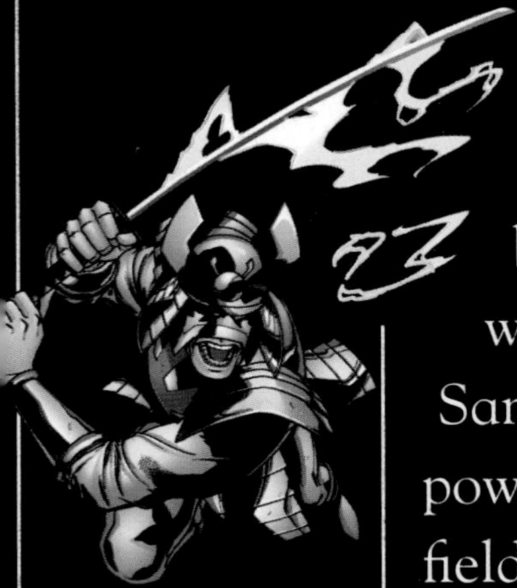

Silver Samurai

At different times, Wolverine both battled against and worked with the mutant known as Silver Samurai. Silver Samurai's mutant power is that he can create a force field which he can channel through his sword for increased power. He is also skilled in the martial arts of bushido and kenjutsu.

This son of a Japanese crimelord used his samurai skills to work as a mercenary. He worked for the evil organization Hydra for a time.

Samurai
Silver Samurai uses a traditional samurai sword.

Big Hero 6
Wolverine joined this Japanese Super Hero team.

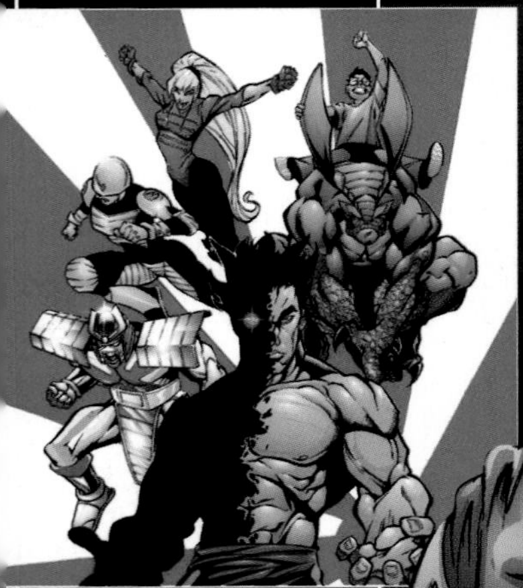

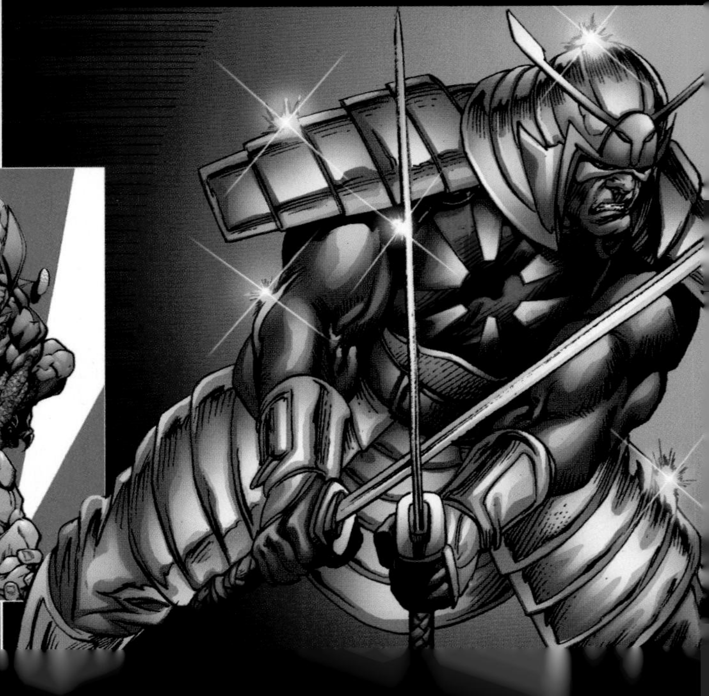

When his father died, Silver Samurai reconsidered his life of evil and joined Japan's first Super Hero team, Big Hero 6. In time, he became the group's leader. Later he returned to a life of crime.

Silver Samurai first clashed with Wolverine when Silver Samurai tried to take over leadership of the family clan from his halfsister Mariko Yashida. Wolverine was in love with Mariko and stopped Silver Samurai's attempt.

Mariko Yashida
Mariko fought her halfbrother Silver Samurai for control of their family clan.

Enemies and allies
Wolverine and Silver Samurai worked together in Big Hero 6.

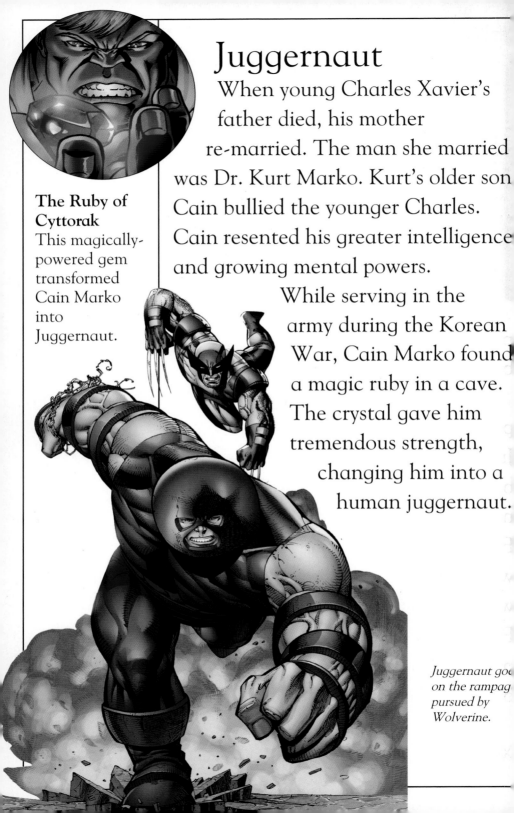

Juggernaut

When young Charles Xavier's father died, his mother re-married. The man she married was Dr. Kurt Marko. Kurt's older son Cain bullied the younger Charles. Cain resented his greater intelligence and growing mental powers.

While serving in the army during the Korean War, Cain Marko found a magic ruby in a cave. The crystal gave him tremendous strength, changing him into a human juggernaut.

The Ruby of Cyttorak
This magically-powered gem transformed Cain Marko into Juggernaut.

Juggernaut goes on the rampage pursued by Wolverine.

Power!
Powered by
the magical
ruby,
Juggernaut
has amazing
strength.

Before he had the chance to use his newfound power, Cain was buried alive in the cave.

Years later he emerged as the powerful being known as Juggernaut. Once Juggernaut begins moving in one direction, no force on Earth can stop him. Freed from the cave, Juggernaut wanted to kill his stepbrother, who by this time had become Professor X. Juggernaut invaded the professor's mansion and was stopped by Wolverine and his fellow X-Men.

In time, Juggernaut joined the X-Men.

Black Tom Cassidy
This heat-blasting mutant turned to crime and joined up with Juggernaut to fight the X-Men.

Apocalypse

Apocalypse is 5,000 years old, making him one of the first mutants ever born on Earth. He has been around since the time of the Pharaohs of ancient Egypt. Apocalypse's abilities include enormous strength and the power to shape-shift. He shares Magneto's belief that humans and mutants cannot live together.

Double threat
Apocalypse has superhuman strength and can change his shape at will.

Shape-shifter
Apocalypse has the ability to turn parts of his body into weapons or change shape to defend himself from harm.

Apocalypse sees humans as unfit and wants to eliminate or enslave them. This puts him in direct conflict with Professor X's views that mutants and humans should work and live together peacefully. Wolverine and the X-Men have battled to stop Apocalypse many times.

Apocalypse's shape-shifting ability makes him a tough opponent for the X-Men. Whatever type of attack they throw at him, he can block with a shield made from a section of his body. Even Wolverine's adamantium claws have trouble slicing through the barriers Apocalypse can put up.

The Four Horsemen
Apocalypse is served by his Four Horsemen. The Four Horsemen are Death, Famine, War, and Pestilence.

Hulk and Wendigo

While wandering in the Canadian wilderness, Wolverine came upon two mighty creatures battling. One was Wendigo, a savage, mindless beast covered in white shaggy fur. Given his power by an ancient curse, Wendigo has enhanced strength, stamina, and reflexes.

Wendigo
Wendigo is the victim of a curse that changes humans into mindless creatures.

Two-for-one
Never one to avoid a fight, Wolverine tackles both Wendigo and the Hulk.

He has sharp claws on his hands and feet, and he is practically indestructible. Wendigo was fighting the Hulk, the huge powerful man-brute.

Still in his animalistic uncontrollable phase, Wolverine leaped into the battle. He slammed into Wendigo with his feet, knocking the creature down. Wendigo's heightened reflexes enabled him to jump back up, but Wolverine slashed at him with his razor-sharp claws. Hulk then picked up Wendigo and threw him into a tree. Wolverine jumped on top of Wendigo to finish the fight.

Wolverine then turned to the Hulk and jumped on top of him, toppling him over. This was to be the first of their many battles.

Teammates
Although Wolverine and the Hulk have fought some epic battles, they have also teamed up at times.

Wolverine vs. Sabretooth

Wolverine has no more deadly opponent than Sabretooth. Sabretooth has the same mutant abilities as Wolverine. He has amazing healing powers and razor-sharp claws.

Adamantium
Like Wolverine, Sabretooth has adamantium attached to his skeleton.

Wolverine and Sabretooth have squared off many times using their remarkably similar mutant abilities. Their battles date back more than a century.

In the early 1900s, when Wolverine was living among the Blackfoot Indians, he fell in love with a young Indian girl named Silver Fox. When Sabretooth saw them together he went berserk with jealous rage and attacked Silver Fox. Wolverine stepped in and a vicious battle followed during which Silver Fox was killed.

Silver Fox
The death of Silver Fox was a major reason for Wolverine's hatred of Sabretooth.

When Sabretooth was working for the Hellfire Club and Wolverine was working for the Canadian government's Department H, the two battled again.

Every year, on Wolverine's birthday, Sabretooth hunts him down. Sabretooth's annual birthday "present" for Wolverine is to defeat him in battle. No matter where Wolverine is in the world, Sabretooth uses his enhanced senses and exceptional tracking ability to find him.

Savage
Sabretooth can survive living in the wild like a savage animal. He lives for battle and revenge.

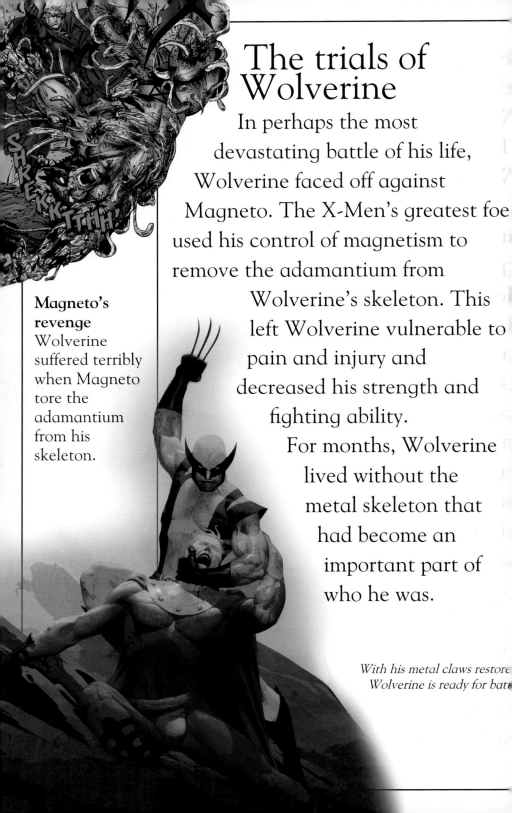

The trials of Wolverine

In perhaps the most devastating battle of his life, Wolverine faced off against Magneto. The X-Men's greatest foe used his control of magnetism to remove the adamantium from Wolverine's skeleton. This left Wolverine vulnerable to pain and injury and decreased his strength and fighting ability.

For months, Wolverine lived without the metal skeleton that had become an important part of who he was.

Magneto's revenge
Wolverine suffered terribly when Magneto tore the adamantium from his skeleton.

With his metal claws restore *Wolverine is ready for bat*

Finally, Apocalypse restored the adamantium to Wolverine's skeleton. Then he made Wolverine his slave.

The complex individual who has gone by the names James Howlett, Logan, Weapon X, and finally, Wolverine, is a walking contradiction. He's part human, part animal. He tries to do what's right, but sometimes ends up on the wrong side. He works hard to maintain his self control, yet can go berserk in an instant.

He's already had a long, and bizarre journey, lasting more than a century. But with his amazing ability to age only very slowly, that journey may have just begun.

The future? Where will the future take Wolverine? No one knows for sure—least of all Wolverine himself.

Glossary

berserk
Out of control.

brainwash
To convince someone
to do something
they don't want to
or believe something
that they really don't
believe.

brooding
In a dark mood.

conspiracy
A plot or plan made by
a group of people.

contradiction
Opposites.

C.I.A.
The Central
Intelligence Agency of
the US government,
concerned with
activities involving
national security.

domination
Control.

electromagnetic
Using electricity to
create a magnetic
field.

espionage
Spying to obtain secret
information.

estate
A large house
surrounded by land.

extraterrestrial
Occurring outside
the Earth and its
atmosphere.

immune
Unable to be hurt by.

indestructible
Unbreakable.

inherited
Passed down from one
generation to another.

instincts
The natural way
someone acts.

intruder
Someone who breaks
into a home.

juggernaut
An unstoppable force.

loner
One who prefers to
spend time alone.

mercenary
Someone who is hired
to fight for a foreign
country.

mutant
Someone with an extra
ability.

mystic
A spiritual leader.

pharaohs
Rulers.

philosophy
A system of beliefs.

refuge
Relief, a safe place.

samurai
A Japanese warrior.

smugglers
Criminals who bring
illegal or stolen goods
from one place to
another.

telepathic
Mental.

teleport
Move instantly from
one place to another.

tropical
Very hot and rainy.

Index